PAUL BUNYAN

by **Maurice Dolbier**

Illustrated by
LEONARD EVERETT FISHER

Random House · *New York*

LEGACY
BOOKS

You Won't Believe It

If you were to hear everything that's been said about Paul Bunyan, you probably wouldn't believe half of it. And you'd be right.

Take the story that says: When Paul lay down to sleep, he rested his head on the Rocky Mountains, and the wigglings of his big toes made hurricanes off the Delaware Capes. Anybody can see that's just a story. It wouldn't be reasonable to believe it about anybody, not even Paul Bunyan. The Appalachian Mountains, maybe, but not the Rockies. No, sir.

Was there ever a real live Paul Bunyan? Maybe so. He might have been a husky young man in a logging camp who did a piece of work that was extra hefty and extra smart. After he moved on to another job, maybe the other loggers kept on telling stories about him. The stories would get bigger and bigger. And they'd spread far and wide, the way this American country was spreading. Pretty soon Paul Bunyan wasn't Paul Bunyan any more. He was all the loggers of all the nation, rolled up in one big package.

Then along came the ink slingers. That's what they called the clerks in the lumber camps. But I'm talking about the people who write stories down on paper, instead of just telling them out loud around a cook stove. When this tribe got wind of the Paul Bunyan yarns, they went to the old-timers, and asked them to tell all they knew about Paul.

Well, any time an old-timer is asked to tell all he knows, he's going to tell quite a lot more than he knows, too. That's the way old-timers are. It's a good thing, I guess. If they weren't, what we call history wouldn't be half as much fun as it is. The Paul Bunyan tales had been getting taller and taller as they were passed along by the boys out in the forests. When the old-timers passed them along to the ink slingers, those stories took on an extra elevation.

One after another there came books about Paul Bunyan. And with every book, the old stories were given new and fancy trimmings. Ink makes things grow, too.

Who was Paul Bunyan? That makes no difference now.

Who is he? He's all the things that everybody said he is.

Who will he be? That depends on you. He'll be the Paul Bunyan of the new stories that you make up about him, and the new meanings that you find in him. He's a part of America, and that means part of you.

All I figure to do right now is to give you some of the stuff that's already in the Paul Bunyan story. Maybe there'll be a little extra stuff along the way. Well, what can you expect? I'm an ink slinger too.

The Baby That Shook the Earth

On the coast of Maine, where the pines meet the sea, the whispering began. It began among the needles of the pines. It went on to the firs and the spruces and the hemlocks, and to the birches and the oaks and the elms. And it went west.

"He's here," the whisperers said. The words went westward through all the uncut forests of the continent. They came at last to the redwoods on the western shoreline.

"We're ready for him!" the redwoods roared. The roar went east. And all the uncut trees of the continent joined in, shaking their branches as if they were shaking fists. Back across the land the booming challenge came. It came at last to the coast of Maine, and roared around the cabin walls.

"It's quite a wind that's blowed up," said the big man standing by the cradle.

Down in the cradle, the baby opened his eyes. He grinned and let out a shout of laughter, and the ground shook as far as the Arctic Circle.

Paul Bunyan was a restless baby. One night, when he was three weeks old, he rolled around in his sleep and made so much commotion that four square miles of woods went down flat.

That sort of upset the neighbors, especially

the ones that owned the woods and the ones that were naturally nervous. So they made up a delegation and went to see Paul's family.

They took a look at the baby. There he was, lying in his cradle and using a big iron chain for a teething ring. He was making a cute cooing noise like Niagara Falls on a stormy day. The neighbors said the things that neighbors always have to say about babies. They said he was a darling boy. They said they couldn't figure whether he looked more like his father or his mother.

In one way, Paul was luckier than most babies. He was so big that not one of those people dared to tickle him under the chin and say "kitchee-koo."

They they got around to saying what they'd come for. They didn't have anything against babies. But the whole blamed State of Maine wasn't big enough for this one to move around in without breaking something. The Atlantic Ocean was more his size. If it was all the same to Paul's folks, would they mind if Paul was set offshore some place for the time being?

Paul's folks said they didn't mind. So everybody pitched in and built a floating cradle. They made it out of some of those trees that Paul had knocked down. Then they got a crane and lifted Paul out of his old cradle into the new one. They tied a strong rope to the new cradle and to six big sailing vessels. They had the cradle towed out to sea and anchored off Eastport.

That night it seemed that everybody might get a good night's sleep for once. It didn't turn out that way. Oh, Paul slept all right. But he kept

Paul's folks tied a strong rope to his new cradle,

rolling around, and you should have seen the tides it stirred up! Well, you can still see them. The ones he started in the Bay of Fundy are going yet. They rise anywhere from 25 to 50 feet, and nobody can argue about that.

Next day people ten miles inland were sweeping the Atlantic Ocean out of their kitchens, and it was decided to haul Paul Bunyan back to land.

As Paul grew up, he was a great help with the chores. Sometimes he needed toning down a mite. All boy children do, and Paul more than most. He

and six big sailing vessels towed it out to sea.

did that time when his father sent him to get wood for the woodbox, and Paul came back with a couple of acres of white pine.

Yes, Paul had to be told some things, and some things he had to learn for himself the hard way. One day, in his early teens, he borrowed his father's shotgun and went out after a bear that had been giving the farmers trouble. He spotted the bear all right, about five miles away. So he let loose with the buckshot. He ran up to see if he'd got the bear. But he ran too fast, and the buckshot hit him in the seat of the pants.

Paul was so quick that he had to be slow, and so strong that he had to be gentle. And these things Paul learned, and took to heart.

The other kind of learning, the kind that comes from books, Paul never did have any luck with. He was always sorry about it too. In later years, whenever he saw his friend Johnny Ink-slinger reading a book, a sad look would come into Paul's eyes. It was as if he'd lost something and he couldn't remember what it was, but it was something good and mighty special.

You see, there was a little schoolhouse up there in Maine where Paul was growing. But he grew so fast that he couldn't get into the building. The school teacher had some books, but the print was too small for Paul to read for himself. When the teacher tried to read them to him, he had to shout so hard and so high that it sounded, way up in Paul's ears, like nothing but a tiny "bzzzzz."

The teacher wanted to teach Paul the ABCs, but he couldn't find a blackboard big enough. So he had to use the side of a slate quarry. He spent five days drawing the letter A on the side of that quarry with a great chunk of chalk. Then he spent four days washing it off. The letter B took him seven days to write and five days to wash off. By that time the poor teacher was dog-tired. Scared, too, because he had no head for heights. So he just gave up, and Paul never learned to read or to spell.

One day Paul and his father had been out in the country lake-fishing. Paul's father was frying the fish over a campfire, and Paul was stretched out over a couple of fields, looking up in a lazy way at the sky. It had that funny orange color that sometimes comes in the twilight.

High up an eagle flew over, heading west. And it sent a call that came floating down to

9

Paul through the air. What did the call say? Well, you've heard it. I've heard it. But it's kind of hard to put it into words. There's something in it that tells you that the world is big and full of adventure. And it tells you to get a move on.

Next day Paul left home, and headed west.

Paul Bunyan, Day Breaker

In the blackness, Paul Bunyan went out of the camp with an axe over his shoulder. He made four long strides that took him to the topmost peak of Ontario's Blue Mountains.

In the blackness, he took a firm hold on his axe and swung it full-tilt at the towering night. The stars trembled, and a few little ones fell. Back came the axe. Then again—wham!—it cut forward. All up and down the eastern sky a little crack came and grew wider.

Once more the axe swung, and on both sides of the crack in the sky the black night fell tumbling down, leaving the way free and clear for the blue skies and bright sun of morning to shine out over the world.

Then Paul hurried back down to the camp,

and let out a shout to wake the loggers. "Hit the deck!" he yelled. "Fire in the mountains!" And by the time he'd finished yelling, usually the daylight had caught up with him.

Another workday had begun.

Well, that's one of the stories about Paul's first real job. Day Breaker for his uncle, who ran a logging camp up in Canada. Maybe it's so. Maybe it's not. Of course, it doesn't sound likely to people who live in a mild climate. But up there where it's cold, maybe the nights do freeze in and have to be chopped open to let the daybreak through.

There's another story about Paul that puts him even further north. It says he invented a device to stretch the days, and sold it to the Eskimos. To my mind, that's carrying things too far.

Chances are Paul Bunyan did work for his uncle, but as a logger. We know he started young at that trade. He'd go through a third of an acre of timberland, taking just four chops at every tree, no matter how big it was. Then he'd fix his axe to a handle made of strong woven grass. He'd stand back, and swing it around, and let it go.

Then he'd stand back and swing the axe around.

And those trees would flop over, as pretty as you please.

He was a good man to have around.

"Let's Fight It Out"

At first the men thought it was thunder rumbling in the south. But as it came nearer and nearer, they figured it was too regular for thunder. It was more like slow and heavy footsteps, and that's what it was. Pretty soon, over the tops of a

The trees flopped over as pretty as you please.

clump of trees at the edge of camp, a man's head
and shoulders heaved into view. The man had a
beard as red as sunset.

The trees went down as the man booted them
out of his way. He came into the camp, and looked
down at the men, and said:

"Who's the boss here?"

Paul's uncle stepped forward and said that
he was.

"You want to take on the best logger in the
world?" said the man. "That's me. Hels Helson!"

"I've already got the best logger in the world," said Paul's uncle. "But the name's not similar."

A funny look came over Hels Helson's face. He reached in his hip pocket and pulled out a big black bear. He put it down on the ground, and it scooted off into the forest.

"Fool critter," said Hels Helson. "Must have crawled in there when I was asleep last night, thinking it was a cave." Then, as if he hadn't heard Paul's uncle at all, he said again: "You want to hire the best logger in the world? Here he is. Hels Helson. That's me."

Then they all heard a noise like thunder rumbling in the north, and everyone except Hels Helson knew what it was. It was Paul Bunyan coming in from work. He came striding along, his big black beard waving in the breeze. Hels Helson opened his eyes up to the size and shape of soup plates.

"Got a stranger here," said Paul's uncle, with a little grin.

"Good to meet you," said Paul, stretching out his hand.

Hels Helson swallowed hard, and then he said: "All right. Let's fight it out!"

14

Reaching in his pocket, Hels pulled out a bear.

Up to that time, nobody had ever thought of inviting Paul Bunyan to fight him. So Paul didn't know what fighting meant, and he had to ask. When Hels Helson told him, Paul laughed so loud that when the echoes came rolling back they knocked over the cook house.

Then Paul said: "Seems to me that's the craziest way of passing the time I ever heard about. There's a lot of good work to be done, and a couple of fellows as big as we are could get it done fast. What's the use in trying to knock each other down when all these trees are waiting for us to do it to them?"

"Just the same," said Hels Helson. "If it's all the same to you, I'd like to try."

"It's all the same to me," said Paul Bunyan.

So Hels Helson tried to grab Paul Bunyan in a wrestler's hold, but he couldn't get his arms around him. Then he kicked him in the shin, and almost broke his own toes. Then he punched him in the stomach, and Paul was just tickled. Hels leaped around, jumping and punching and kicking and wearing himself out, and it didn't have the least effect on Paul.

At last, Hels Helson backed up half a mile, put his head down, and came running in like a wild bull. He rammed into Paul so hard that he knocked himself out.

When he came to, he pulled himself up with a grunt and shook Paul's hand. Then he turned to Paul's uncle and said:

"You want to hire the second-best logger in the world? Here he is. Hels Helson. That's me."

And it was done, and Paul and Hels became fast friends from that time on.

16

The punch in the stomach just tickled Paul.

Johnny Inkslinger

One day when Paul was out cutting lumber for his uncle, he came upon a tree that was extra tough, and it took him a full ten minutes to fell it.

"Timber!" he yelled, and the tree went smashing down.

A little while later, he heard "Timber!" but he thought it was an echo, and didn't pay any attention. Then the tree he'd just cut down came zooming up again and fell down the opposite way. It missed his head by inches.

"What in thunderation!" Paul said, and he went over through the woodlands to see who'd thrown the tree back.

He found a man sitting in a clearing, muttering something with his eyes closed. The man was taller than Hels Helson, almost as tall as Paul Bunyan, but a good deal thinner than either of them. He didn't have a beard, and he wore glasses. His clothes were mighty peculiar to find up there in the wilderness—a dark gray business suit and a high white collar.

"Twenty three hundred and sixty-four," the man was saying, "and take away five hundred and eighty, leaves one thousand seven hundred and eighty-four. Now isn't it fine that it comes out that way? Who'd ever have thought it?"

"Excuse me, mister," said Paul Bunyan, "but did you just throw a tree at me?"

The man opened his eyes.

"A tree came down here while I was figuring," he said, "and almost knocked the figures out of my head. I just tossed it back without looking. Glad there was no harm done. My name's John Inkslinger, and I'm from Boston, Massachusetts.

A man sat in the clearing with his eyes closed.

Did you ever hear of a subject called algebra?"

Paul shook his head.

"That's good," said the man. "I was thinking of inventing it, and it's no use inventing things that people have heard of. Let's see now. X plus Y squared equals A divided by B and multiplied by C. How's that?"

"Sounds all right," Paul admitted. "What's it mean?"

"I don't know yet," said the man. "But one of these days I will, after I get around to inventing the stuff. What's your name?"

"Paul Bunyan," said Paul. "I work for my uncle. I'm a logger. I should judge by your get-up that you're not."

"No," the man said. "I'm a figurer. There's too much noise down in Boston. So I came up here where I figured I could figure in peace."

"How do you figure?" Paul asked.

"You fool around with numbers," said the man. "You know what numbers are?"

Paul shook his head.

"Never heard of numbers?" the man said. "My, this is a wild country, for sure! Pull up a hill and sit down, and I'll explain them to you."

So that's what Paul did, and Johnny Inkslinger talked and taught. By the end of the day, Paul could figure, too, up to putting one and one together. He wanted to keep on learning, so he asked Johnny why he didn't take a job at the lumber camp. Johnny asked about the wages.

"What are wages?" said Paul.

"How much money does your uncle give you for working for him?" asked Johnny.

"What's money?" said Paul.

Johnny did some more explaining, and Paul put one and one together again. Right then and there he decided to go into business on his own.

Paul Bunyan and Company

For this business of his, Paul took Hels Helson on as his foreman and Johnny Inkslinger as his bookkeeper. Then he moved west again—west by south—back into the States.

He hired more men as he traveled.

He hired two cooks: Sourdough Sam and Hot Biscuit Slim.

He hired a blacksmith: Big Ole.

He hired a crew: Swede Charlie, Chris Crosshaul, Joe Murfraw (there were two Joe Murfraws; this was the one named Pete), Shot Gunderson, the Little Chore Boy (he was only twelve feet tall), and those mighty brothers the Seven Axemen (nobody knew where they came from, and when the brothers were asked, they always pointed straight up).

Paul Bunyan's company was almost complete.

One day they came to a lake, and the cooks went down to draw water for the coffee. Just as they dipped their pails in, all the water in the lake disappeared.

They looked down the shore and saw a big blue ox just swallowing the last gallon. They led the ox into camp and measured it. It was seven and a half axe handles wide between the eyes. To be exact, seven and a half axe handles and a plug of tobacco.

The blue ox took to Paul right away. It went over and nuzzled its nose in his hand and made a low friendly bellow like thirty-three bass fiddles scraping away all at once.

"Hello, Babe," Paul said, and that was the ox's name for then and for ever.

The company was complete.

Paul Bunyan's Been There

Wherever you go in this big country, you're likely to find somebody who'll tell you that Paul Bunyan's been there. Been there and done things. Like digging the Great Lakes so that Babe would have watering troughs that wouldn't run dry, or digging a canal that turned out to be the Mississippi River.

You'll hear that the dirt he threw off to the right became the Rocky Mountains, and the dirt he threw off to the left became the Appalachians.

You'll hear that Kansas used to be full of mountains before Paul Bunyan came. He turned it upside down. Now it's flat as a pancake because all its mountain peaks are inside the ground, pointing to the center of the earth.

You'll hear that Paul got so sad at what he saw going on in New York City that he fell to crying, and his tears started the Hudson River.

Western deserts or southern swamps, eastern shores or northern forests, Paul is said to have been there and done things. And if by chance you can't find any stories about his having been in your neck of the woods fix some up. Everybody else has.

Right now, let's stick to the northern forests, because we know for sure that Paul was there. Paul and his men and the Blue Ox. They logged all through Michigan and Minnesota and the Dakotas, North and South, and they were always pushing westward to where the redwoods waited.

Flapjacks for Breakfast

Maybe you'd like to know what life was like in those lumber camps of Paul Bunyan?

Well, the day started when the owls in the woods thought it was still night. The Little Chore

Five men skated up and down on the griddle,

Boy would blow his horn, and the men would tumble out of their bunks for chow.

There were always flapjacks for breakfast. These were made on a big round griddle about two city blocks wide. Before the batter was poured on, five men used to skate up and down and around on it with slabs of bacon tied on their feet. It'd take an ordinary man a week to eat one of the flapjacks that came off that griddle. Paul used to eat five or six every morning.

After breakfast came the work. The loggers tramped off to the woods. One crowd cleared the paths, another cut down the trees, another cut them

with great slabs of bacon tied on their feet.

up into logs, another piled them on carts or sledges. Then Babe the Blue Ox hauled the carts down to the water.

Soon after sunset, the men would all be back at the camp for supper. That was either baked beans or pea soup. Sometimes the cooks would surprise them, and serve pea soup or baked beans.

Sourdough Sam never liked to work very hard. One time he just dumped some split peas in the lake and then boiled the lake water and served it.

Matter of fact, Sam didn't stay with Paul Bunyan long. The men didn't mind that he was lazy, but they got almighty tired of sourdough. That's a kind of fermented dough that rises like yeast, and Sam used it in all his recipes. He put it in the coffee one morning. The Little Chore Boy drank a cup, and then started to rise into the air and float across the lake. They had to lasso him and pull him down.

After supper, they'd sit around and talk and sing and tell yarns so whopping that you'd never believe them.

Then, about nine o'clock, they turned in. Of course, it wasn't all work at Paul's camp.

26

The men would hunt and fish, and sometimes they'd have log-rolling contests. That's when you stand on a log in the middle of the water and start the log rolling under you, trying to keep your balance as long as you can. Joc Murfraw used to win, mostly. Paul Bunyan himself never took part, except to demonstrate, because nobody could beat him anyway. He used to get the logs rolling so fast under foot that they set up a foam solid enough for him to walk to the shore on.

Cold, Snow and Ice

These are the things that went on fairly regularly, but I couldn't tell you what a typical day at Paul's camp was like. No day was typical. They were all special, and so was the weather.

There were fogs so thick that you could cut houses out of them, the way they do with snow and ice in the far north.

There were winds that blew up and down and in every direction at once.

There were thaws so quick that when the snow melted it just stayed there in big drifts of water for a week.

27

There was one time when all four seasons hit at once, and the whole camp came down with frostbite, sunstroke and spring fever.

There was another time when the rain didn't come from the skies at all. It came up from China, away underneath the world. Up from the ground it came, first in a drizzle and then in a pour, and it went straight up into the air. It got the sky so wet that the clouds were slipping and slopping around in the mud for a month.

But most of the stories you hear are about the winters that Paul Bunyan's loggers had to put up with. No one ever had winters like them before or since.

The cold was mighty intense. It went down to 70 degrees below zero, and each degree was 16 inches long. The men couldn't blow out the candles at night, because the flames were frozen, so they had to crack the flames off and toss them outdoors. (When the warm weather came, the flames melted and started quite a forest fire).

It was so cold that the words froze in mid-air right after they'd come out of people's mouths, and all the next summer nobody had to talk. They had a winter's supply of conversation on hand.

28

The cold wasn't the only thing that was peculiar. Sometimes the snow was too. One winter it came down in big blue flakes, and Johnny Inkslinger used the icicles to write down the figures in his books. That's how he got the idea for inventing fountain pens. And the men used to have snowball fights until they were blue in the face.

Then Came Mosquitoes

Yes, the weather did all it could to upset Paul Bunyan's operations. And when the weather gave up, the mosquitoes tried.

One spring day, the men were working in a swamp, near a lake in northern Michigan, when they heard a droning noise. They looked up to see the whole stretch of western horizon black with flying creatures heading right toward them. The men didn't stop to inquire. They dropped their tools and went hot-foot back to the camp and locked themselves up in the bunk house.

Pretty soon they heard a terrible racket overhead, and then long things like sword blades began piercing through the tin roof. Paul Bunyan grabbed a sledgehammer and began pounding those stingers flat, so the mosquitoes couldn't get in or out. The rest of the mosquito army saw that it was no use and flew away.

Paul figured they'd be back with some new ideas, and he'd better have a new idea, too, just in case. So he sent Swede Charlie on a trip down into Indiana. He'd heard they had a special kind of monster bumblebee there. Charlie brought some of these back, and Paul trained them to fly in a protective circle around the camp. He thought that the next time the mosquitoes came they'd have a surprise. They did, and he did too. The bumblebees and the mosquitoes liked each other so much that they married and had children, and the children grew up with stingers in back and in front.

You won't hear anyone say that Paul Bunyan was ever stumped by any problem that came up. I won't say so, either. But that section of timber-land up in Michigan was the only place that Bunyan's men moved away from while there were still trees to be cut. I suppose they got a better offer.

Rivers You Never Heard of

No, nothing that Paul Bunyan and his men met up with was ever like the things that ordinary

Paul began pounding the stingers flat.

When Babe the Blue Ox let out a loud bellow,

men have to deal with in this world. The weather was ornery, the mosquitoes were ornery, and the rivers. . . .

Well, one of them was named the Ornery River. Paul's crew got the logs in and began to drive them down-river. After they'd gone a few miles, the river turned around and started back toward camp. Paul was there. When he saw the whole kit-and-caboodle heading his way, he brought Babe the Blue Ox over to the bank, and told him to bellow loud. When the river heard the noise, it was so scared that it turned around and ran in the right direction.

But it was still ornery. It became curious about

the river ran in the right direction again.

what was on the other side of a mountain on its left bank. Without giving a word of warning, that river started to climb the mountain. The logs couldn't make it, of course, and they just piled up at the foot of the mountain. Well, luckily, when the river reached the top, it didn't see anything of interest. So it came galloping down again, hit the logs, broke the jam, and went on its way behaving itself. But it could have been a really bad situation.

With the Big Auger River, the situation was always bad. That wasn't because you didn't know what the river was going to do, but because you did. Maybe in these days when people press buttons or pay somebody else to do their work for them, nobody knows what an auger is. It's a tool for boring holes, and it moves in a spiral, like a corkscrew. That's just what this river did. The fish that swam in it became shaped like corkscrews too. They wouldn't nibble at a worm, but if you threw a cork in, you were pretty sure to catch one.

You can see the trouble there'd be trying to float logs down the Big Auger. By the time they came out at the head of the lake, they'd be reduced to plain sawdust. Paul built a cement dam across the river, trying to tame it. But the Big Auger bored right through the dam. Paul finally had to have Babe pull a mountain all the way down the river and flatten it out.

Then there was the Big Onion River. The first part of the name was wrong. The stream was hardly big enough to get a dozen logs in, and hardly fast enough for the logs to move more than a dozen inches in half an hour. But the water did smell powerfully of onions, and garlic grew on the shore. Before they'd been working there long, Paul Bunyan and his men shed so many tears that the river became a wide and roaring torrent.

According to the stories, there were lots of

34

rivers with strange names and stranger behavior:

The Rubber River, that wasn't a river at all until Paul and Babe stretched it into one.

The Big Fraidy River, that was scared and had to be pushed.

The Hot Water River (when it ran between cliffs of soapstone it changed its name to the Big Bubbly).

The Daytime River, that stopped flowing every night when the sun went down.

Oh, there were lots of them, and Paul Bunyan licked them all. Anyway, all but one.

The Round River Drive

This was in Michigan too. Bunyan's men had finished one of their biggest logging operations. A hundred million feet of logs were in the river, and the whole crew joined in the work of driving them. They'd been gone four weeks when one day Hels Helson let out a roar.

"Look over there on the bank!" he said.

They looked, and they saw a logging camp that was as big as Paul Bunyan's. They called out, but nobody seemed to be around. Whoever had been there must have finished all their work and started driving their logs ahead of Bunyan's men.

"I didn't know any other loggers were in this part of the country," Hels Helson growled.

"Neither did I," said Paul.

"Looks as though they'd done a complete clearing of the land," Johnny Inkslinger said thoughtfully.

"Yes," said Paul. "Somebody's done a good job."

"Somebody's done a quick job," said Hels Helson. "They're going to get their logs to the mill before we do."

"Good for them," said Paul. "We're not going to get ours there at all if we just stand around talking. Let's move!"

They got the drive under way again, and again they'd been four weeks on the river when Hels Helson let out another roar:

"I'll be a swoggle-horned sunfish! Look over on *that* bank!"

They looked, and they saw another logging camp that was as big as theirs and the one they'd come across before. It was deserted like the other. This time Paul was worried. He called to his men:

"That's two big camps we've passed. If we run into another, we're sunk. Why, when we get our drive to the mill, the price will be down to thirty cents a thousand. That's not worth all the work we're putting in. Maybe we'd better go ashore and talk it over."

So they went ashore. While the rest were talking, Hot Biscuit Slim walked over to the camp kitchen. He wanted to see if there was any food that he could sling together for lunch. Pretty soon he came back, laughing like a loon.

"Stop that cackling," said Johnny Inkslinger. "This is serious business."

"You don't know how serious," Hot Biscuit Slim said, wiping his eyes and giggling. "This here is our own camp!"

"What?"

"I left a letter from my pappy under the nutmeg grater, and there it is still! This here river we've been driving is as round as a doughnut!"

The Round River Drive, folks call that adventure. It's one of the Paul Bunyan stories that everyone agrees really happened.

But nobody agrees on what happened next.

The folks that won't allow that Paul Bunyan

was ever beaten give all kinds of ways that Paul beat Round River:

He put sourdough into it and made it rise and find a proper channel.

He hitched Babe to the water and broke the river apart.

I say that Paul Bunyan shook his fist at the river and laughed at himself. The river laughed back, and Paul Bunyan said:

"What have you got to laugh about? You're not going anywhere at all, and I am!"

And he went.

Come to think of it, I guess that story, too,

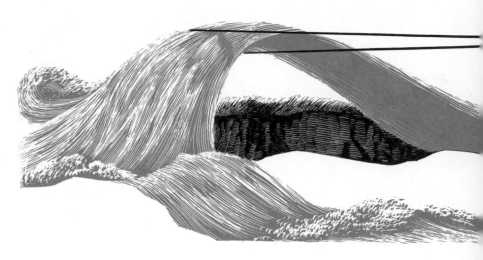

Paul hitched Babe to the water,

shows that Paul Bunyan wasn't beaten, not even by Round River.

Strange Animals of the North Woods

As Paul Bunyan made his way through the forests of the North, he had, and he met, some of the strangest animals that ever lived.

Of course, none of Paul's animals was as useful as Babe, the Big Blue Ox. But his men were partial to Lucy the Cow. She gave chocolate, vanilla and strawberry milk. But she ate so many evergreen trees that the milk began to taste of white

and the ox broke the river apart.

pine. Then the men used it as a cough medicine.

Benny, the Little Blue Ox, was more trouble than he was worth. He grew two inches every time you looked at him. And he was so fond of flapjacks that he often ate all that were ready for the men's breakfast. His greed got the better of him, and he swallowed a red-hot stove, and nobody was sorry.

The camp had two dogs, Elmer and Sport. Elmer was a terrier. Most terriers can catch rats. Elmer was the only one that could catch moose.

Sport was part elephant hound and part wolf, and a sad thing had happened to him when he was a puppy. One of the men heard a noise at night and flung an axe in its direction. It cut poor Sport right in two. Paul Bunyan was a good hand at first aid, and he put Sport together again. But in the dim light he made a mistake and sewed the back half on upside down. This made Sport better than new, because now he was a reversible dog. He could run on his front legs for a while and then do a somersault and run on his back legs. That way he never got tired. He was the greatest hunting dog a man ever had, not only because he could run faster than any other, but because whenever the animal he was chasing turned around it would drop dead in its tracks from laughing.

Part of the adventure of logging in those northern woods in Paul Bunyan's day was the assortment of creatures you might meet there. Part of our good luck in living when we do is that now those creatures are extinct. Some of them, like the Dismal Saugus of the Swamps and the Happy Hodag of the Hills, made each other extinct. I don't know how the others went, but I'm mighty glad they've gone.

There was the Dreadful Whirling Wimpus (or Wampus), that moved so fast no one could tell what it looked like.

The animals would turn around and start laughing.

And the Wild Teakettle, that whistled before it struck.

And the Side-Hill Dodgers (or Winders), that had a set of short legs in front. The men rode them to get up the sides of hills.

And the Wiskerwoo Bird, and the Snow Snake, and the Bog Hop, and the Goebird, and the Agropelter, and the Snow Wasset (in the summer it was called the What Wasset), and a hundred others, not forgetting the Mammoth Rabbits that terrorized the wildcat population.

Good riddance!

Paul Tries His Hand

The stories about Paul Bunyan weren't confined to the lumber camps. Men in other lines of work liked Paul so much that they decided to adopt him. I can't answer for the facts, but this is the way some of the stories go:

Paul Bunyan was a driller in the oil fields. Once he drilled so deep he went right through to China. Another time he struck a gusher that gave floods of buttermilk. And once he struck a dry hole, pulled it up, cut it into sections, and sold the sections as post holes to farmers.

42

Paul Bunyan was a farmer. One of his cornstalks grew so high that Swede Charlie climbed it, and so fast that he couldn't get down again.

Paul was a construction worker. He dug the St. Lawrence River and Puget Sound and anything else you care to mention.

Paul was a surveyor. He was a Forest Ranger. He was a cowboy. He even went into the hotel business. The hotel he built was so high that the top floors had to be put on hinges so the moon could get by.

Paul was a shipyard worker. He was a soldier. I guess if you were to go by all the stories that have been told about him, there isn't much that Paul wasn't.

Except an ink slinger. I'm glad he left something for the rest of us to do.

The Mountain That Stood on Its Head

With all the peculiar jobs that Paul Bunyan was called upon to do, it's not easy to pick out the oddest one of all, but I'd be inclined to give the prize to this one. It came about when he was logging in the Dakotas.

One day Hels Helson came loping back to

camp. His eyes were popping, and he was so excited that he could hardly speak. When he did speak, he didn't seem to be making any sense. He was talking about trees growing backward and a mountain standing on its head.

Well, they ducked his head in the cold water of the lake, and they gave him three gallons of black coffee to quiet him down. Then they told him to begin again, and he did. He talked about trees growing backward and a mountain standing on its head.

So Paul Bunyan figured that he must mean it. He asked Hels Helson to show him. They went about ten miles from camp and turned a corner; and there it was. Smack in the middle of the landscape was a mountain whose peak was stuck in the ground. Its big round base was miles high in the air, and on its sloping sides there grew some of the finest standing timber Paul Bunyan had ever seen. But all the treetops pointed down.

Now Bunyan's men could do a lot of things, but moving around upside down like flies wasn't one of them. So Paul had to contrive a way of getting at those trees. What he did was to fill a double-barreled shotgun with sheets of steel. Then

The steel from the shotgun brought down the trees.

he knelt at the bottom, took aim up along the sides, and shot. The steel bit through the tree trunks, and the trees fell. After that, it was easy.

It's no use looking for that mountain. It isn't there any more. Snuffling around where the mountain came out of the ground, Babe the Big Blue Ox found some delicious grass and started to eat it. Now, Babe never knew his own strength or his own appetite. Without thinking a thing about it, he chewed right through the solid rock. The mountain was tipped off balance, and it came smashing down on Babe and the whole countryside. What's left of it we know today as the Black Hills. But that was the end of Babe.

"Time We Were Moving On!"

Paul Bunyan stayed in the Dakotas for some time after that, doing no work, doing nothing but mourn for Babe. His men were uneasy, seeing the change that had come over their leader and friend.

Johnny Inkslinger tried to distract him by inventing checkers, dominos, and plane and solid geometry. Hot Biscuit Slim tried to comfort him with fancy dishes like cream puffs and Eskimo pies. But nothing had any effect.

Then one day an eagle went by, high above them, flying west. A call came floating down that only Paul Bunyan could hear and understand.

He splashed cold water on his eyes. He pulled up a pine tree and combed the tangles out of his black beard. He slapped Hels Helson hard on the back. And he said, "Time we were moving on!"

And they moved on, through Montana and Wyoming and Idaho, to the place where the redwoods waited, and the land ended, and the great work would at last be completed.

What Became of Paul Bunyan?

On the continent's west coast, the redwoods met their master, and bowed and fell before him.

What happens to a hero when the heroic job is over? What happened to Paul Bunyan after the forests had been tamed, after the Age of Wood had vanished and the Age of Steel arrived?

The question has been answered a hundred times, and each answer has been different. Some say he married and settled down. He went to Mexico, to China, to Russia. He went to the moon and found fine stretches of uncut timberland on the dark side. He's still somewhere in America's northwest. Two stories I take no stock in: that he became a big businessman, or that he died. No. Not Paul Bunyan.

I guess that there's room for another answer—the one hundred and first.

It was at the last camp and in the hour before sunset. Hels Helson had been out in the woods working with the Seven Axemen. He came back to the camp alone, and he looked more shaken than the Little Chore Boy had ever seen him.

"Where's Paul?" he said.

47

The Little Chore Boy jerked his thumb in the direction of Shadow Mountain.

"He went up there a while ago," he said. "All by himself. You reckon he's feeling up to snuff these days?"

"Why shouldn't he be?" Hels Helson snapped.

"Well, he's not been doing as much work as he used to, and I just thought. . . ."

"You'd be a lot more use if you gave up trying to think, and did your own work right for a change," Hels Helson said and strode away toward the mountain.

"Now what's eating him?" the Little Chore Boy thought.

Paul Bunyan sat beneath a tall pine and looked out over the rich Oregon land, to where the first red line of the Pacific Ocean gleamed under the setting sun. He heard the trees snapping behind him, and knew, without turning, that Hels Helson had come.

"Boss," said Hels Helson, "I hate to bother you, but I thought you'd better know."

"Yes?"

"It's the Axemen. They've gone."

Paul Bunyan turned. He ran his fingers

"He went up there a while ago," said the Chore Boy.

through his beard, which was still mostly black, although in places it shone silver.

"Where did they go?" he asked.

Hels Helson said nothing. He pointed straight up. Paul Bunyan nodded.

"I guess I always knew they'd leave us one

day," said Paul. "And the day came. They were a good crew. They'll be missed."

He looked away again toward the distant sea. Hels Helson stood on one foot and then on the other, waiting for Paul to say something else. He didn't, and Hels started to walk away. Before he'd gone far, Paul's voice stopped him:

"Did you hear that sound just now?"

"What sound?"

"Far away. Sort of like an ox bellow. Sort of like Babe the Blue Ox when he was hungry and supper was late."

"I didn't hear it," said Hels Helson unhappily. He waited a minute, and then he went, and he couldn't explain the feeling he had that he'd just said good-by.

The Tree Must Be Felled

There were long red and gold streamers of cloud in the western sky, and riding above them the clear star of evening. An eagle circled over Paul's head, and the call came down.

Paul got to his feet, not as nimbly as he had done in the old days. He picked up his axe and slung it over his shoulder, and he followed the call. Not west this time, for the West held nothing but the open sea. Paul wasn't even thinking what direction he was going. He just followed.

The way went upward, and then the way went downward, and Paul stumbled along it. He was more tired than he ever remembered being, so tired that after a while he just closed his eyes. He moved on until the night came, and then he gave up. He stretched out on the ground and slept.

When he awoke, the sun was up, but the fog was so thick that its light hardly came through. Paul looked around him. What little of the country he could see was like no other country he'd ever seen in all his life. There were spindly trees and huge gray ferns and prickly bushes with black berries drooping from them, and the ground was soggy. But the night's sleep had done Paul good, and he felt happy and strong. It was the way he had felt when he was a young man and knew he had a good job waiting for him.

There was a job waiting now. Paul didn't know what it was, but he felt it waiting for him off there through the fog. He whistled a lively tune of the logging camps and walked on.

Sometimes the ground gave way, and he sank in water halfway to his hips. Sometimes he heard sounds of hissing and laughing in the gray unknown that surrounded him. But he went on, feeling stronger by the minute.

And at last he came upon the Tree. For a time, all the strength and happiness were drained from him.

The Tree stood on a big patch of solid ground. It towered higher than any tree he'd seen anywhere, but it wasn't its height that made his blood freeze. The trunk of the Tree was thick and green and running with slime. Its branches writhed like snakes, and its fat pale leaves whispered foully.

For only a minute Paul Bunyan stood without motion. Then he stepped forward and swung his great axe. It bit into the Tree, but as soon as he drew it out and swung to hit again, the wound in the Tree was healed. Again and again he hurled his axe against the Tree with no effect. The laughing sounds around him grew louder.

Then Paul Bunyan realized that this was the Tree of Evil, and that the only way it could be felled was by striking at its roots. He threw his axe down and began tearing at the ground with

Paul hurled his axe against the Tree with no effect.

his bare hands. As he hurled away great clumps of earth, and the hidden roots began to come into view, the mocking laughter faded, then died away altogether. He worked on in a sudden and heavy silence.

The silence was broken by a sloshing in the swamps. Paul Bunyan looked up from his work, then stood and shouted and waved his arm. Out of the fog, the Seven Axemen came, and each was grinning. Close by, an ox's bellow sounded, and a big blue shape loomed toward them.

"Fire in the mountains!" yelled Paul. "All together now! Let's get this one down!"

And Paul and Babe and the Seven Axemen started the job that they're working on still. No telling how long it'll take, because the Tree of Evil keeps sending down more roots all the time. But what a day it'll be when Paul Bunyan yells "Timber!" and that Tree comes crashing down!

Legacy Books